# Pips in the Wind

## in the Wind

### Stories and Allegories Reflecting on the Fruits of the Spirit

CATHERINE WOOD

authorHOUSE®

*AuthorHouse™ UK*
*1663 Liberty Drive*
*Bloomington, IN 47403  USA*
*www.authorhouse.co.uk*
*Phone: UK TFN: 0800 0148641 (Toll Free inside the UK)*
*    UK Local: 02036 956322 (+44 20 3695 6322 from outside the UK)*
*www.fruitofthespirit.uk*

*Published by AuthorHouse 05/27/2021*

*ISBN: 978-1-6655-8857-7 (sc)*
*ISBN: 978-1-6655-8858-4 (e)*

# CONTENTS

# INTRODUCTION

When the apostle Paul wrote to the church in Galatia, he encouraged his listeners to let God's gentle Spirit flow through their lives. The fruit of that would be love, joy, peace, patience, kindness, goodness, faithfulness, gentleness, and self-control.

These stories reflect on each of the fruits of the Spirit, particularly in the light of the growing global awareness of our urgent need for change in order to protect and care for our planet. The hope is that they will contribute to a deepening spiritual awareness of God's compassion for all life on earth as we nurture and grow our fruits of love, respect, and concern.

By our wounds
we wound one another.

By His wounds
we are healed.

# 1

## LOVE

Paddy wanted to look his best, but his hands were shaking so much he could hardly manage to do up his shirt buttons. Nine years it had been. Nine long years of silence and absence, a wretched void where once there had been his son.

It all seemed so petty now, but at the time, what they had fought over seemed so desperately important. An ethical standing of ground, though perhaps it had really just been a territorial battle—two stags, hardened against their antlers, fighting to the death of their friendship. Paddy had made certain that he drew first and final blood. But in the end, he had ripped out his own heart as his son had gone, leaving the wounds of supremacy to weep.

Now, though, he had heard from an old friend that his son would be passing through late that evening. He would have to change trains at the station and wait half an hour. Paddy fumbled with his buttons, his stomach lurching with excitement—and fear. What if it all went horribly wrong? His son had sent no word that he would be so near. Ghoulish fantasy conjured a scene at the station of derisive rejection in front of a crowd of sniggering onlookers, the old stag finally fallen and crawling away to die. Yet even with hope so honeycombed with dread, he had to try. He just had to.

It was a twenty-minute walk to the station. Paddy left with an hour to spare. The churning swirl of painful memories, apprehension, and longing left him nervous and restless. It was better to be moving. It would be easier to wait at the station. At home his anxiety would bleat about early trains and treacherous timetables.

The steady rhythm of walking through the dark and the shadows of familiar landmarks on the way helped to ease the knots in his stomach. He had just passed Berry's hedge when he heard a loud scuffling behind him. Paddy smiled. Hedgehogs. He had lived among trees and animals all his life. Often when sleep abandoned him, he spent the night in the woods, taking food to the furry and prickly ones that had become his family.

The scuffling came closer, and Paddy stopped. There was something about it that felt far from right, an urgency that pleaded with him to listen more carefully. Then suddenly a hedgehog crashed out of the undergrowth and scurried over to Paddy. She scratched frantically against his shoe, ran a few feet towards the hedge, scuttled back to Paddy, and then back to the hedge.

Paddy followed, crawling through a small gap that children had made playing hide-and-seek. Bits of spiky hedge tore through his hair and whipped his face and arms as he dragged himself through. The hedgehog watched, waited, dashed ahead a bit down the narrow space between the two rows of bushes that formed the hedge, and then turned to make sure that Paddy was following.

It was a slow, painful crawl, but now Paddy could hear other sounds—the high-pitched squealing of a baby hedgehog in distress. He followed the sounds to where the mother was waiting beside her baby. He had become hopelessly entangled and trapped within a thorn bush that had grown inside the hedge. He was terrified and bleeding where some of his prickles had been ripped out in his frantic attempts to free himself. But he grew calmer as he began to sense that this huge animal beside his mother was there to help.

With hands torn and aching, Paddy finally managed to disentangle the baby. 'I'd take you home and do what I could for the torn prickles,' he apologised, 'but I have to go now and meet my son.' The baby hedgehog snuffled against his hand, and all Paddy could do was pray that he would heal.

It was impossible to turn around in the hedge, so he had to back out, tearing his shirt on the way. Out on the road once more, he sighed heavily and tried to sense how much time he had lost. At least half an hour. Still, he had given himself an hour more than he had thought he would need. There was still plenty of time.

Around the next bend, Paddy turned onto his much-loved path through the wood. No one else would have thought of it as a path, but many years earlier the trees had taught him a different way to listen on sleepless nights. They had shown him a way to walk among them that kept him from treading on small plants or trampling some tiny animal's home. With the light of the full moon playfully tossed among their branches, he could see the way ahead quite clearly and began to feel more at peace about the baby hedgehog. At least he would now know to stay well away from thorn bushes.

He almost walked straight into it, an intricate, delicate but lethal work of art abandoned by its eight-legged weaver but still intact enough to have snared a bumblebee in its stickiness. Her desperate attempts to break free had only entwined her further. Now she was exhausted; she had strength left for only the feeblest of struggles.

Paddy looked at her helplessly. Any other time he would have stopped, freed her from the spider's tomb, and settled in for the painstaking process of unravelling each thread. It was always a long process because of having to be so careful not to tear a wing or pull out a leg. Paddy knew that he could not stop for long. Not this time. As he freed the bee from the web and laid her in the grass, he could feel the tears prickling behind his eyes. 'I'm so sorry,' he told the sticky, furry ball, 'but I have to go and meet my son.'

The bee kicked feebly and tried to roll over. But her legs were stuck together, and her wings were glued to her back. For a moment, Paddy wondered about ending it for the bee, but as he raised his foot halfway, he felt sick and stumbled on down the path instead. How could he even think of killing a creature he knew he could help—if only he had time.

Time. Paddy went on another few steps, the warring tension inside turning to acid in his throat. He *did* have time; the station was only ten minutes away. *But you might miss him!* the fear inside screamed. Yet a deeper, quieter voice turned Paddy back as though there had never been a breath of doubt. With two tiny bits of twig, carefully agonising, he slowly unwound each strand of web from wings and legs, his smile breaking free with five legs, then six, then the first wing. The other had been slightly torn as the bee had struggled. As he laid the bee back in the grass, Paddy prayed that she would still be able to fly.

He half ran along the path now, trying to sense how much more time he had lost. Every breath seemed like a rehearsal for eternity. Twenty minutes? Half an hour? Perhaps even longer. Still, he was not that far away now. Perhaps the train would be late. Perhaps. Perhaps.

Gradually, the trees thinned, and before him Paddy could see the shortcut path over the hill that led down to the village and the station. A surge of adrenalin nearly knocked him off balance as his heart began to race. Nine years of silence, of absence. Soon, for good or ill, it would be over. Even one hour ago it had seemed like a dream, but now with the village so close, it was abruptly, powerfully real. As trepidation suddenly gushed through widening cracks in his resolve, Paddy gripped his knees, gasping. Fear would have turned him back, but the pounding in his chest pushed him on through the last trees and out onto the path. Almost there.

Paddy knew that bark. Even in excited recognition and relief, old Jock's bark was unmistakable. He had been missing for three weeks, and Paddy's friend Arthur, who lived on the other side of the valley, had almost given up hope of finding him. Paddy stopped and called, and Jock came limping from the bushes where he had been hiding. He was thin, his paws cracked and bleeding, but his tail was wagging hard enough to start a dust storm. Paddy knelt and patted him, then ruffled his fur as he stood up to go. 'Come on, old lad. You'll have to come with me to the station, but later I'll take you home.'

Jock limped a few paces after Paddy and then collapsed on his haunches, whining. Paddy tried to coax him but realised it was hopeless. Jock's paws were shredded, and walking on feathers would have been too painful. 'I'll just have to carry you,' Paddy told him. But even half starved, Jock was a solid, heavy dog, and Paddy could barely lift him. They tumbled in a heap together. As Jock licked his face, Paddy began to panic.

'What am I going to do?' he asked Jock, despairingly. 'I can't just leave you here. If you manage to wander off, we may never find you again. Sorry, old boy, I can't take you with me. But at least if I tie you to a tree, we'll be able to come back for you later.' As Paddy reached down to undo his belt, he suddenly felt as though a cannonball had crashed-landed in his stomach. He had changed his trousers and put on his best pair—the pair without a belt.

Plunging into the trees, Paddy searched frantically for anything to use as a rope: a thin springy branch, a bit of vine, anything. With tears of despairing frustration stinging his eyes, he groped around in the dark, feeling the seconds slipping into minutes, passing him by like life rafts just out of reach of someone drowning. Suddenly his hand brushed against something ropy. He tugged furiously at the old root but finally had to chew through it to get it free.

With a sickening sense of betrayal, Paddy led Jock back to the bed he had made in the bushes and tied him to one of them. 'I'll come back for you. I promise,' he told the dog. As he stumbled back onto the path, trying to shut out the despondent howling behind him, Paddy could only pray that Jock would go to sleep—a long, forgetful sleep.

Paddy gasped a deep breath and ran. Even trying to imagine how much time he had lost was unbearable. His hands and clothes were torn, but he no longer cared. All that mattered now was simply to get to the station before the train left. He tried to be calm, to remember that his son had half an hour to wait between trains. 'Even if I can just get there in time to see him as he's leaving,' he groaned to himself. 'Even if he just knows that I wanted to see him.' Paddy slowed to a fast walk, his breathless chest pounding. 'Even if the train's leaving, perhaps I'll be able to shout and wave and he'll hear me.'

Paddy half fell over the ridge and started running down the slope to the station. But even between his own rasping breaths he could hear a child's cry coming up the hill towards him. A small girl, about seven years old, was running, stumbling, as breathless as he felt himself. 'Please, please,' she called to him, 'you've got to come! My dad's in the swamp, and he's drowning. Some horrible men beat him up and pushed him in, and I can't get him out by myself. He's too heavy for me and the swamp's sucking him in and please, you've got to come. Please help me.'

As her waves of terror and panic crashed over him, something in Paddy suddenly went deathly calm. There was no hope of seeing his son now. The swamp was at least ten minutes away. By the time he got back to the path, the train would be gone. Drained of all but numbness, Paddy followed the girl, his misery giving wings to her resuscitated hope.

As they came near to the swamp, Paddy could just make out a shape in the water on the far side, but nothing was moving. As they ran round to him, it looked to Paddy as though they were too late. The man was big and heavy with the sucking weight of swamp water. Yet between them, with the combined strength of her desperation and his inner silencing of any more pain, Paddy and the girl managed to drag him out.

Pain, though, had jarred the man back into consciousness. As he looked at his daughter in the moonlight and then at Paddy, for a moment his choking breathing stopped. Then he whispered, 'Dad? Dad, it's me.' As Paddy looked closer, numbness kicked off its blankets in sobbing relief as, through a newly grown beard and the mud that was glued to his face, he recognised his son.

Sometime later, when the doctor had been and gone, Paddy listened to how they had arrived on an earlier train as he wanted to show his daughter the places he had loved as a child while it was still light before taking her to meet her grandfather. How they had been attacked, and he had been badly beaten while trying to protect her. How good it was to be home, and what a pity about his letter which Paddy had never received.

After a while, Paddy got up. 'Where are you going?' his son asked.

'I'll be right back,' Paddy answered. 'There's something urgent I have to do.' And as he reached for the phone to let Arthur know where he could find his dog, Paddy's hands began to shake. For if not for the gifts of a wounded hedgehog, a dying bee, and a lost dog, at that very moment he would have been sitting at the station. Waiting. Waiting …

There are times
when it feels as if

now

has no mercy,
and so we dream …

# 2

## JOY

'It's going to be a wild one tonight,' the shopkeeper said, pulling her coat a bit tighter around her as though in anticipation.

'Aye, you're right about that,' the farmer replied, nodding. 'Best be seeing to the woolly ones. They won't like it, though, all this toing and froing.'

In the end, the sheep barely bleated. They had sensed what was coming long before even the most experienced of their minders and knew that the heavy trek up hills and over stones would bring them to soft grass, trees, and shelter. On this tough, rugged farm it was an area of unexpected beauty, yet something about it had always puzzled the farmer. There was a network of holes weaving through the trees, but never once, in all the years he had lived there, had he seen a rabbit.

Months earlier, curiosity ruffled, he had even camped for a few days in a hidden patch between three of the trees, certain that he would finally see some of the tunnelling inhabitants. The first two days had been fun, with the lure of unravelling a complicated mystery, but the baffling had eventually given way to frustrated boredom. 'Silly old thing,' his daughter had jibed fondly, ruffling her father's thinning hair. 'If you were a wildlife photographer, waiting for something rare and exotic to show itself, it would be worth your aching joints. But rabbits?'

'I know,' he had answered ruefully. 'But I really would like to know what's up there. There's something very strange going on under those trees.'

❧

'You *know* it's forbidden! Why can't you accept that? Do you *want* to turn into something evil-smelling and disgusting?' Emily had more than enough of her youngest daughter that day, and her patience was feeling as raw as her paws.

It had been her turn to scrape the warren's droppings into the dung burrow and seal it off. But in the dark she had pushed too far into a retaining wall, and part of the tunnel had collapsed in on her. Sorrel, her daughter, was supposed to have been helping her. As usual, she had been nowhere to be found, and it had taken two painful hours of digging and scraping before Emily managed to burrow her way out.

By that time, the tiny speck of light filtering through one of the vent holes in the neighbouring tunnel had been a relief.

Usually she would have scurried past it, paws over her head lest any light touch her and turn her into something obscene. Life was full of fear for the rabbits of Woodhaven Warren, and there was nothing they feared more than sunlight.

No one could remember a time when light had not been a source of terror. Every week the whole warren gathered to listen to the stories of what had happened to those who had been reckless enough to go above ground during the day. Many years earlier, a dog from a neighbouring farm had been hiding amongst the trees. He had killed and half-eaten a young rabbit that had been too intent on a tasty tuft of grass to sense the danger in time. Her friends had dragged her down into the burrow in youthful trust and hope the older rabbits would make her well again. Instead, they had been so horrified that they had forbidden the young ones ever to go above ground again. They all stayed huddled in the darkest, safest corners they could find for weeks afterwards.

Gradually, as weeks festered into months, the story of one rabbit's misfortune had fermented into a potent brew, a lethal mixture of truths and half-truths increasingly soured by others' fears and shadows. Eventually, what had happened to one rabbit, and the ghoulish imaginings about what would happen to every other rabbit, had become indistinguishable.

Somewhere from the bowels of stricken memory other stories had surfaced, only adding to the growing dread and hatred of anything above the ground. Entrance passages had been closed off, vent holes had been sealed, and in the stuffy safety of total darkness, open air had become the enemy. Sunlight had become abhorrent, and sunrise the greatest evil of all. For any rabbit to see a sunrise would be instant death. Rumour self-seeded, and as the stories were told and retold, the dog was forgotten. It was daylight that had changed a young, healthy rabbit into a maimed and hideous travesty. Fears were flayed with tortured imaginings of what they would be turned into if ever they went above ground.

Finally, suffocation had forced the vent holes to be reopened, but no rabbit of Woodhaven Warren ever went to the surface during the day. At night, a small team of specially trained foragers went outside to gather grass, their eyes covered with hoods. An old rabbit had once asked whether moonlight and starlight were bad as well, and a potentially disastrous debate had been quashed only just in time. If rabbits started thinking that they were safe at night just because the sun was asleep, there would be moves among the restless, difficult ones to be allowed to go to the surface after dusk.

That could not possibly be permitted. Anything might happen to them. They might stray too far from the burrow and be caught by the rising sun. They might lose their way altogether. They might feel dew on their paws and wind in their whiskers. They were disruptive and difficult enough to control as it was. It was much better that they believe that *any* kind of light, except that in the Hall of Lights, to be dangerous. Hopefully they would value their lives enough to leave the stars alone.

❧

The Hall of Lights was a strange, eerie place at the junction of three tunnels. Some weeks after the young rabbit was killed, before the vent holes had been reopened, a wise older rabbit had realised that if they never saw light of any kind they would eventually go blind. It had been hard to convince the others, but finally they had reluctantly agreed to let her reopen the five vent holes above the junction. They had then been covered with moss and bracken, allowing only a pale, patchy light to seep through.

Each day the rabbits spent just long enough in the Hall of Lights to keep their eyes from dying. Then they raced— or were chased—back into the darkness. Sorrel, however, had discovered a little offshoot tunnel. When no one was watching, she would squeeze in and hide, wait until everyone had gone, and then sit, staring raptly up at the moss-covered holes. She ached to know what was happening to her, but there was no one she could talk to. Even the others who kept scratching at their parents' resolve to keep them away from the surface could not help her. For them, the arguments were a way of testing what was solid and what was fluid, what was immovable and what could be pushed. Sometimes it was just a good way of creating a little whirlpool in an otherwise stagnant day.

Like the others, Sorrel had heard all the ghastly stories before her eyes had barely opened. She went dutifully to the Retelling Gatherings each week, but somehow a part of her remained shielded from the fear, untouched by the terror. With every dark-clad day, that part of her was growing stronger. Torn between what she was being told by those she loved and what something deep inside was whispering to her, the Hall of Lights had become her only place of peace. Hidden in the shadows, her fear-soiled mind felt rain-washed, while her eyes opened another kind of vent hole in a heart falling in love with forbidden light.

As her sore and weary mother had been finally swamped with irritation at yet another plea to go to the surface, Sorrel had fled back to her only sanctuary, trembling and confused. Never had she felt so restless, so panic-stricken, so desperate to be free of stale air and shadows. She lay panting in a little pool of the strongest light, trying to gulp in quietness and calm, yet wishing miserably that rabbits could cry.

❧

A few days later, screeches ran the gauntlet of every tunnel's echo. 'Don't listen. It's all lies. It *has* to be. He's a demon disguised as a rabbit. He'll lead us to our deaths. He's evil, a curse. Stay away from him. Drive him out!'

No one could even imagine where he had come from. The old, greying rabbit had suddenly appeared at the entrance of one of the passages used by the night foragers, asking for a place to rest for a while. The rabbit on guard duty was stunned, scarcely believing he was hearing a rabbit's voice—outside, in daylight. At first the guard had hunched down, silent, but the wandering rabbit only called more loudly. Soon every rabbit in the warren knew he was there.

Finally, one of the elders went to the entrance to talk to the stranger, to try to scare him off. Not believing that he could possibly be a rabbit, the elder told him what would happen if they opened the tunnel entrance before dark. For a while there was silence outside. Then the stranger's sad voice seemed to whisper into every vent hole, through every sealed entrance, through even the pores of the earth itself: 'There's nothing to fear out here. It's safe. Darkness is good, but so is daylight, and the sun warms your fur. In the dark you can rest, and in daylight you can run and play and see all the beauty of trees and flowers. Come out and see, or your safety will become your grave.'

Within minutes, the elders' enraged screeches drowned out the whispers. When finally they stopped, the stranger's voice was silenced. Believing they had been seduced by a fiend from hell, new horror stories flourished in the fresh dung of their nightmares. Baby rabbits were guarded more closely than ever. But for Sorrel, it only enflamed her yearnings. From then on she spent every moment she could in the Hall of Lights as though only there could she hold on to a tiny thread of sanity.

Then one day as she sat gazing up at the light holes, earth suddenly began to fall onto her face, and bits of moss and bracken landed in her fur. As she watched, her eyes growing bigger and wider, the hole grew bigger and wider. A nose appeared and then whiskers and ears, until finally, a whole head pushed through. Soft eyes blinked at her.

'Hello,' the old, greying rabbit whispered. 'I thought you'd be here. Are you ready to come?'

Later, Sorrel had scarcely been able to remember how she had been freed. As though in a dream, she had listened to the stranger burrowing, watched him burst through into the Hall of Lights, and finally had followed him out into the daylight she had been taught to fear and despise.

As she sat shivering, paws over her eyes, all the stories she had ever heard stormed like a hurricane through her memory. They threatened to suck out her vital organs while light changed her into something hideous and grotesque. Gradually, though, as the old rabbit simply sat with her, she realised that she still had paws and a tail, and the rabbit who sat smiling at her was the most beautiful animal she had ever seen.

In a delirium of joy, she rolled in the grass, chased him through the trees, and watched in amazement as a butterfly landed on a flower and a bee smothered her legs with pollen. Exhausted, Sorrel collapsed in a happy heap beside him. 'Tell me about the rest of the world,' she said. 'I want to see everything, everywhere.'

The old rabbit laughed, and the hours melted away as he painted pictures in her mind of the vast grandeur of forests, the lush greenness of open fields, the magic of sunlight sparkling on water, and the mystery of moonlight stretching a silver pathway across the sea. He told her of other animals and birds—high-flying things, and tiny crawlers and climbers. Most of all, he helped her imagine the glory of sunrise as they sat under the starlight and waited for the dawn.

Then, as the newborn sun edged over the horizon and darkness dissolved into red and gold, awed silence evaporated Sorrel's last residue of fear. She knew that she had been born for this day alone. Finally, she turned to the grey rabbit and whispered, 'You must live for each new day just to be able to see this again.'

'Not exactly, little friend,' said the old rabbit, sadly. 'With my insides I feel it, and with my heart I see, but all my life I have lived as you have lived—in darkness. Tell me what you see, little one. Share your eyes with me. For you see, I am blind.'

Though the winds of love
may have died,

I will face today
in full sail.

# 3

## PEACE

*(In honour of all who were evacuated.)*

Some years ago, a little boy named Raphael lived on an island with his mother. It was a very small island; few people lived there, but those who did were friendly and peace-loving. Life was gentle and at one with the waves.

Raphael's mother had created a garden from his father's grave, a garden of groves and sheltered places, fields full of flowers, fountains, and ponds. The tears of a woman's broken heart had been returned to the earth, giving birth to a blessedness that the earth gave for her healing and for the life of all who might come.

And everyone did. From his first hours beyond the womb, Raphael grew with the sounds of birds and other children's laughter, bubbling water and the animals that came to drink.

Some friends had two legs, some four, and others too many to count. Fear was a poisoned berry that everyone knew not to eat.

Raphael's mother taught him, through her silence, to listen with his heart. Each day among the trees, and at night with dreams touched by the sounds of the nocturnal ones and the waves, he learned to understand more deeply the mystery of the love that holds all things in being. Day by day he wrapped his simplicity in the mantle of its power. Each day he helped his mother care for the garden by listening to each plant's need. When spring woke the flowers, he somersaulted with their colours across the sand. When trees settled for their winter rest, he watched the sea through their nakedness, quiet inside. He and the earth and the sky were one, and the love that embraced them was the warmth at the heart of the seed of all life.

Then one day the boat came, bringing a piece of paper from the government many miles away. 'All children must be educated,' it read. 'Isolated children especially. They must be sent to school.'

Raphael's mother was distressed. There was no school on the island. The man on the boat knew that. He had come to take them. 'Don't worry,' he told the islanders. 'I'll bring them back when it's holiday time. It will be good for everyone. They'll learn things that will help you raise your standard of living.'

The man on the boat took the children away, and Raphael's mother cared for the garden alone. People still came and sat in the garden, but without the sound of children's laughter, the garden shared their sadness. Some flowers remained only buds that spring. 'Never mind,' the island people told each other. 'They'll be home soon.'

They smiled at one another outwardly, but each was secretly thinking, *Yes, but then they will have to go again.*

One day, after a stormy night had left lots of driftwood on the beach for their fires, someone looked up and out to sea. At last, it was the boat, returning. As it neared the shore, they ran into the waves, laughing and dancing as happy children jumped out of the boat and into their arms. That night they lit a big fire on the sand. Everyone sat around it so that they could be warm while the children told them what they had learned.

'We're learning to read,' said one.

'Will that help you?' asked her mother.

'Of course,' replied her daughter, a vague hint of disdain in her voice. 'If we can read, we can get to know so much more than what we ever learned about here.'

Her mother was quiet. She stared at the sand, wondering, *You may gain knowledge, but will wisdom come with it?*

An older boy said, 'I'm looking forward to next term. We're going to start geometry.'

'What's that?' asked his father.

'It's about shapes and lines and points. And how they fit together.'

'Does that help you understand the patterns of the stars?' asked his father, interested.

'No,' laughed his son. 'That's all just superstitious nonsense. Geometry's about squares and triangles.'

His father looked out to sea, disappointed, watching the waves curling and spiralling around the rocks.

'I've been learning to add up,' said another of the girls. 'Then you know how much things cost when you go to the supermarket, and you can make sure you've got plenty of money.' Many of those listening wondered what a supermarket was, but no one quite managed to ask.

'What did you learn, Raphael?' asked his mother.

'Nothing much,' Raphael answered, throwing sticks into the fire.

'He's having to learn to stand up for himself,' joked one of the other boys. 'Aren't you, Angel Face?'

The next day Raphael's mother surprised him under one of the trees in the garden, where he was working intently at something.

'What are you doing?' she asked.

Startled, Raphael was not able to hide it as he had begun to hide things at school. 'I'm making a bow and arrow,' he mumbled.

'What are they for?' his mother asked.

'Target practice.'

His mother looked at the green, bleeding branches in his hands. 'Did you forget to ask the tree if you could have the branches?' she asked quietly.

Raphael said nothing. His mother stared at him as he stared at the ground, pulling bits of bark from the branch. 'The earth is in our hands,' she said. 'It is for us to touch gently.'

The few weeks passed quickly, and the boat came to take the children back to school. Their parents stood on the beach and waved until they were out of sight. Then they slowly went back to their work. Raphael's mother sat with the injured tree and then walked gently between the beds of flowers. Some had dropped their petals before time. Few of the children had come to play in the garden. Some said they had too much homework, despite it being the holidays. But it seemed their laughter was about something else now.

The months passed, and suddenly, there again came a shout from the beach. Everyone rushed down to greet the boat, glad the children were home after so long. They ran into the waves and waited for the children to jump out of the boat. But the children waited until the boat had been pulled right up onto the sand. Even then, some complained about getting their feet wet. That night they lit the fire. Everyone sat round it so that they could be warm while the children told them what they had learned.

'We're doing history at the moment,' said one. 'All about wars and battles, and how some people were spies, and others got their heads chopped off.'

'Yes,' said another. 'It's great. We have war games with each other. Anyone you shoot is dead.'

'Why?' asked the boy's mother, aghast.

'Because he's the enemy,' another replied.

'But why is he the enemy?'

The boy was excited, impatient. 'I don't know. It doesn't matter. He's the enemy. I have to kill him before he kills me. Raphael's really good at it, aren't you Goldie Locks?'

'I'm really looking forward to economics next year,' said the girl whose mention of supermarkets had been a lesson in bewilderment. 'You learn how to get a good return on your investments.'

'On your what?' someone asked.

'Using money to make lots more money without all the hard work so that I can buy all the things I need.'

'Who *does* have to work for it?' her father asked.

'I don't know,' said the girl defensively. 'It doesn't matter. That's just the way things work in the real world.' Then she said brightly, 'I'll bring you back lots of presents next time that will make life better and easier for you.' Her father said nothing and huddled in his blanket. For some reason not even the fire was keeping him warm.

As the days passed, Raphael spent a lot of time alone among the trees. His mother missed him and was deeply troubled at how many trees were wounded and in shock. When she asked him about it, Raphael just muttered and said, 'Target practice,' and walked away.

Then one day she heard a scream and ran panic-stricken in search of the cry. There, lying in some crushed flowers, was a rabbit, an arrow through his heart, the life-light in his eyes dulling into death. Raphael's mother knelt in the ruin and wept for the life that had been taken, and for her son.

As the daylight faded, she carried the broken animal into the grove and returned his body to the earth with her tears, praying for healing to take the place of despair. 'The earth is in our hands, my son,' she whispered. 'It is for us to touch gently.'

Each term the children went back to school. Each time the boat returned, their parents went more and more apprehensively to meet it. As the years passed, fewer and fewer children returned to the island for their holidays. Some sent messages, saying they had too much work to do; others, that they had been invited to stay with friends. Those who did come back looked bored. They complained and demanded things their parents had never heard of.

Few of them ever bothered to visit the garden. The laughter of children was gone, and though many flowers recovered with Raphael's mother's care, some lost hope and died. The grove lay stricken and desolate. In the fifth year of their leavings, Raphael had taken an axe and cut down many of the trees. He had built himself a house away from his mother's tortured, questioning eyes. That year not only the flowers died.

Then one day, with the boat's return, Raphael, too, came only as a message: 'He has joined the army,' it said. 'He will do well. It's being said he's officer material. Plenty of ambition and drive; he can outshoot anyone. You should be proud.'

With each passing year the boat's returns were fewer, but occasionally someone had news of Raphael. 'He's heading for the top,' one said. 'He's got his own command. He's one of the military's bright boys. Angel Face, they call him. God's on our side.'

The people of the island huddled together in stunned disbelief. The boat had come yet again, this time bringing only another piece of paper from the government. 'You are to be evacuated,' it read. 'This island has been requisitioned for military purposes. You are to leave immediately and will be relocated.'

Raphael's mother sat with the others, staring at the ground, eyes seeing nothing. She alone had recognised the signature at the end of the piece of paper.

The island's people were taken away. 'Goodbye,' fell over the edge of the precipice and into the abyss below. Hell came as a nuclear warhead and blew the island away. 'Great shot,' said a young officer, congratulating his commander. 'First rate bit of target practice.'

Far away, relocated and never able to return home, Raphael's mother began the slow, painful task of creating a garden from the grave of her son who had died, a garden of groves and sheltered places, fields of flowers, fountains, and ponds. The tears of a woman's broken heart had come to trust this strange land, giving birth to a blessedness that the earth gave for her healing and for the life of all who might come. Over the grave of the child who had been Raphael she whispered, 'The earth is in our hands, my son. It is for us to touch gently.' And as she planted the final tree in what would grow to be the grove, something shuddered in Raphael as he took aim, and for the first time since he had taken a bow and arrow to fight in defence of his name, he missed.

As we offer our hope
for the cynicism of others,

our wounding
for others' pain,

our attempts at trust
for others' despair,

then together
we will walk the path of redemption
with the One who has dared to trust us.

# 4

## PATIENCE, LONG-SUFFERING

Everyone knew that the street holes went down into the sewer. It was attic knowledge, safely locked away with other discarded mental debris. Like railway conveniences, holes in the street were just one of those distasteful things in life. Avoidance was the twin of discretion.

At least they all had lids. If the sun was shining in the proper sort of way, and if you didn't absolutely have to go to la Boutique de la Belle Cuisine and pass the one right outside, you scarcely noticed them. The thought that one might be left uncovered was unthinkable. The mere fact they were there was distressing enough to delicate sensibilities. The idea that someone might go down one, leaving the hole gaping to announce the iniquity, was outrageous. It was enough to send anyone with breeding groping for smelling salts and aspirin, and the restoration of quietude in a warm bubble bath with a pink gin.

Everyone knew where the holes in the street led, but everyone knew that their town was clean and decent. Tedious unpleasantries were never left uncovered, so when the nice new man people hadn't had time to get to know very well yet fell down one and disappeared, they decided not to worry. They assumed that he had just gone to visit his elderly mother. Surely he would have arranged for someone to trim his hedge and mow his lawn. After a week, though, when four new shoots were quite conspicuously disrupting the hedge-line's aesthetics, and there were, horror upon horror, buttercups appearing in the grass, enough was enough. The council workers were called in and the eyesores of uninvited growth removed.

❧

The smell was awful. Aidan huddled against the wall, listening to trickling sounds oozing damply in the distance. He tried to recover a sense of the last few minutes. He had been walking home in the dark. Suddenly, there had been nothing under his feet. Burned into his memory was the short, sharp fall. Then fresh night air had suddenly become acrid, seeping into shrinking pores. He had felt around for a few moments to check that the pain would only be a bruise. Then had come the disbelieving dawning of realisation of what must have happened and where he was.

The worst had come as he had fumbled for a ladder, some way out. There had been that terrible, scraping clang that had smothered his panic-choked shout. The offending access to the undignified had been covered in the name of the council and deodorised life. Some were oblivious to the despicable in their subterranean task, but the workers' union stipulated fifteen minutes for tea. And who wants to sit guarding a gaping great hole in the street during a break?

Aidan lost any perception of hours in the darkness. He vaguely wondered about morning and evening above, but there was no unfed cat to worry about. Like hope of release renewed with each dawn, inertia fed on the anticipation of rescue. It lay in wait, expecting the uncovering, the breaking in of light and fresh air, the smiling and apologetic faces, and the hero's welcome home. Insidiously it fed Aidan the fantasy that someone had noticed he had disappeared; that somebody would care. So mentally clutching his survival manual and memories of, 'If you are lost, stay where you are,' he settled into foetal dependence. With Mother Earth so readily rubbished, and now surrounded by the foetid gurgling of a womb-full of wastes transplanted into her body, his already little world began to shrink even further as he waited to be reborn.

Aidan detested rats. As a child he had seen one, dead and bloody, gazing blindly up at him from the gutter. From that moment they had been, for him, the most nauseating of all obscenities. He had strongly supported the, 'Death to all rats by the end of May,' campaign. He had obsessively kept his poisonous vigilantism along the sides of the flower bed, in spite of all those who had told him that rats only steal from the starving and were long extinct in their town.

Aidan knew about rats with the intimate fear of one persecuted by a recurring nightmare. So when the trickling sounds merged into scratching, and in the dank dimness he saw something move, revulsion left no niche for doubt. This was a sewer. Something that moved in a sewer could only be a rat.

Whatever it was stopped and sniffed the air. And then it crossed over to the side where Aidan was already stiffening against the wall. He could still not see it with any clarity. Only by not looking directly at it could he make out the dark shape and halting scuttles as it cautiously came nearer, backed away, came nearer, and then backed away again. It could almost have been a beckoning movement, one that invited him to follow, but Aidan was aware only of tension climbing the high-wire within. As one oppressed by a lifelong siege of shadows and about to be finally overcome, anger suddenly drew force from panic. As the animal approached, he lashed out, kicking it viciously down the tunnel.

He heard the dull thud as it hit the wall and what may have been slowly retracting claws slithering down the stone. Then nothing. Aidan sighed his applause at the unveiling of relief only to find it a memorial plaque. For no sooner had he settled into something like a doze, there it was again. The dark lump's strange approaching-withdrawing movement was bringing it gradually nearer and nearer. Anger gained confidence through the animal's hesitation, and this time the kick was more surely placed. More punishingly timed.

With the malicious satisfaction of repressed vengeance released and relieved, he pressed his back against the wall, another son of omnipotence. His certainty that it was dead was as assured as the Philistine's bet on Goliath. He had barely begun to revel in his victory when there it was again—a slow, inch-by-inch approach. As an ebbing tide straining to reach one of its stranded creatures, it seemed to crawl forward, as though mocked in its futility by forces unseen. Aidan watched it for a while, until nonchalant power, bored with teasing broken prey, decided it had enough. This time his kick's intent was to be certain that he would rest in peace.

❧

How long it took the dove to drag herself back through the sewer and out into the pastures above none could say. The girl who lived nearby found her, shock and anger mingling with the heartache this time. She took the dove home and watched over her, cleaning her wounds and waiting for forces unseen to hold or to yield. Part of her hoped this time would be the last.

When finally she returned the dove to her tree to be found by the others, they had all known that this would not be the last time. For each time that she was able to recover, they knew that as long as there were tunnels of death in the earth, and holes into them into which any creatures could fall; as long as a way out was her home and her freedom their hope, she would go the way of the sewer rat, down to where only rats ever go lest any should recognise her in the darkness and follow her home.

When the creatures of the night
have fallen silent
and the last bird has sung,
perhaps, finally, we will awaken
to the depths of our loss.

# 5

## KINDNESS

Tom had plans. For months he had pushed and bullied. Finally, the elderly couple had given in and sold him the three acres of wild land they had never built on. Now he would have it cleared and build his dream house with swimming pool and sauna.

There was just one small problem. The woman next door had filed an objection to his planning application, but Tom was sure that he could sort her out. Though tedious, the ancients had eventually given in. He was not going to let another old fossil get in the way.

As Tom walked along the boundary, making mental notes of all the trees that would have to come down, he could see Sophie watching him from her side of the fence. As he drew closer to her, a surge of frustrated anger suddenly erupted within him.

It had taken so long to get this far, and she was all that stood between him and his dream.

Tom strode the last few steps, fists clenched at his sides. 'I suppose you're the one who's put in the objection,' he snarled. 'This is *my* land, and I can do what I like with it!'

Sophie stood quietly watching him for a moment. Then she calmly asked, 'In what sense do you believe you own a part of the earth that will be here for at least as many millions of years after you've gone as before you were even born?'

Tom's eyes widened in disbelief. He was a chief executive, used to the minions competing to attend to his every whim in the hope of advancement. Who was this crazy old fool to talk to him like this? Unable in the moment to think of a cutting-enough insult, Tom simply turned and walked away.

Almost out of earshot, he heard her call, 'Would you be interested in a deal?'

This was language he understood. Tom slowly wandered back, deliberately making her wait. 'What sort of deal?' he asked suspiciously.

'For five days and nights, come and stay on this land,' she replied. 'Watch. Listen. Listen for the God within you. Simply be here without distractions, without imposing anything. I will feed you and provide for your needs. If, at the end of that time, you still want to clear it and build your house, then I will withdraw my objection.'

Tom stared at her. Five days? Was she nuts? He had far too much to do. Just sitting around looking at the trees he was going to have chipped would be a ridiculous waste of time. Yet if that were all it would take to force her to back off, it could be worth it. It would save possibly months of fighting her in court. Five days? It would be a bit like scout camp. He might even be able to remember how to put up a tent. 'Okay,' he said, 'you're on. I'll book the bulldozers for this time next week.'

❧

The morning after his first night, Tom tapped on the door of Sophie's caravan. 'Come on in,' she called. 'Beans and eggs on toast sound all right?'

Tom, who never normally had time for breakfast, thought it sounded wonderful, but he just murmured, 'Sure.'

'How did you sleep?' Sophie asked.

'Terribly,' answered Tom. 'Some beastly thing was making a racket outside the tent, and then something kept plopping on the roof. Anyway, I'm off for the morning. Too much to do to sit around here.'

'Sorry,' Sophie replied. 'That's breaking our agreement. Five days and nights, without distractions.'

'But what am I supposed to do, just sitting around here?' Tom fumed, frustration rising like an overflowing drain within him.

'Just that,' answered Sophie. 'Sit. Listen. Listen to the God within you. Simply be here.'

Tom clambered over the fence and flopped down under a tree, struggling to contain his anger. *Just think of sitting in the*

38

*sauna,* he told himself. *Just get through this week, and then you can give her beans!*

He closed his eyes, imagining how it would all look in a few months' time. When he opened them, he saw a robin just a few feet away. Tom knew about robins from Christmas cards, but he had never seen a live one. Fascinated, he watched as the robin hopped closer, put her head to one side, flew up into the tree and down again, this time coming even nearer. 'Hello,' Tom heard himself saying. 'What are you doing here?'

'A pair of robins live in that tree,' Sophie said as Tom told her about it over dinner. 'They've been nesting here for years. Last year they had four young ones, and all but one survived.'

'What happened to the other one?' asked Tom.

'A car,' answered Sophie sadly. 'They go so fast. She had only just learned to fly and couldn't get out of the way quickly enough.'

Tom went slowly back to his tent. That evening, sitting beside his paraffin lamp, for the first time since he had been a child he listened to the birds as the light faded, a hymn to the simple goodness of being alive that stirred a sudden memory. It echoed a yearning that left an ache his heart had all but forgotten.

'How was it last night?' asked Sophie, piling his plate with beans and mushrooms on toast.

'Okay,' answered Tom. 'Something that looked huge went past outside the tent, but it was probably just a shadow.'

'You may find that it's real today,' Sophie replied.

As Tom sat with his back to the tree, the sun warm on his face, he heard a scuffling sound. Just a few yards away two fox cubs were playing with their mother, biting her tail and pouncing on her back. He moved slightly. They raced into the bushes but soon peeped out again. Tom sat very still, hardly realising that he was barely breathing. After a few minutes, they came out again, playing hide-and-seek in the long grass. As Tom watched, he slowly became aware that, for the first time in a long time, he was smiling at something other than a breakdown of his company's profits.

∾

At the end of that day, Tom lay awake in his tent far into the night, listening to the sounds of darkness—the gentle rustling of wind in the leaves, snuffling and rasping. Every so often a hoot and a squeal. Then silence. Deep, penetrating silence.

'Tell me about your childhood,' said Sophie as she buttered a third round of toast.

'I can't remember anything,' replied Tom immediately.

'Try,' Sophie gently probed. 'Take your time.'

In the peacefulness of Sophie's caravan, his hands warmly wrapped around another mug of tea, Tom began to tell her about his high-flying father and all the new jobs he had—better money, each time with a bigger house and car. As Tom went quiet, Sophie asked, 'And how many times did you lose *your* home?'

Over the next two days, embraced by the trees and kept company by the wild ones, Tom learned to release the tears he thought he had buried with the lonely boy he had been. Every so often, an ant would scurry over his leg, or a winged one would land on his arm. And when a spider, smaller than a pinhead, crawled across his hand, Tom realised that the tears had changed. Held in a moment of awe, he knew that if something that tiny could be alive, then life itself was vastly bigger than anything imaginable. For all that he had lost and had been trying to recover, he was being shown the way home by all whom he would have made homeless without a thought.

As the final day dawned, Tom watched as the beans slid onto his plate. With an embarrassed grin he asked Sophie, 'Would you be interested in a deal?'

'What sort of deal?' smiled Sophie.

'A little weekend wildlife retreat venture for those who never have time to stop. I think you know the sort of thing—sitting, listening, listening to the God within. I'll put up the tents if you'll feed them. There's just one thing though.'

'What's that?' Sophie asked, laughing inside.

Tom, squirming, answered, 'I really don't like beans.'

The harshest of deserts
are not those where there is only sand,

but those in which there are
little pools of enticing, promising water
that evaporate on sight.

# 6

# GOODNESS, GENEROSITY

The neighbours had watched with mixed feelings as the man had his field dug over, and the trellises had gone up. 'Good grape-growing land,' he had been told, 'as long as you can wait the four years it takes in this part of the world for the vines to grow.'

For most, such a wait was impossible, so his wheat-growing neighbours knew he must be wealthy. They were not surprised to see vines going in. Grapes were a lucrative crop if you were not dependent on what your fields produced from year to year. What *had* surprised them had been seeing him plant a little fig tree at the end of one of the rows of trellises.

'Why is he putting a fig in with the grapes?' they had asked the caretaker.

'Too much good living, most likely.' The caretaker had smiled. 'You need a good dose of figs to push it all through.'

As the years passed, the vines wrapped themselves around the trellises while the fig tree grew taller, with more branches and leaves. Then the year came in which the vines produced their first grapes. As the fruit swelled with moisture, they swelled with pride, feeling the weight of their bunches of grapes growing heavier each day.

One of the vines looked over to the little fig. 'Where's your fruit?' it asked.

The fig tree was quiet for a moment. She had hoped for some fruit, but the vines sucked up so much of the soil's nutrients. So she answered, 'It's not my time yet. Fig trees grow slowly. We put our roots deep into the soil and make sure that our branches are strong enough to hold our fruit, even in stormy weather.'

The vine on the trellis two down from the fig sniffed and stroked its plump grapes with its leaves. 'That all sounds quite tedious to me. Surely the whole point is to produce fruit as quickly as possible. What's the point of roots and branches if you end up with no figs?'

That year the weather was kind, and the vines did well. The landowner was pleased. For a first yield it was good, and the wine it was made into was among the best. He was rather disappointed that there had been no fruit on the fig tree, but thinking it might be a bit soon, he looked forward to the next year.

Months passed as the earth rested, and then there they were again—small, hard little clumps that would soon swell into succulent grapes. As they began to ripen the vines looked across to the fig tree. 'Where's your fruit *this* time?' one demanded.

The fig tree flinched. Her roots and branches had grown a little, but the vines had taken even more of what the soil was able to give, and there had been too little left for her to fruit. 'I'm not ready yet,' she replied. 'My roots have gone deeper, and my branches are getting stronger, but I need more time.'

'Fig trees must be so weak and pathetic,' said the vine scornfully. 'We were able to produce loads of grapes in our first fruiting year while you just sat in the ground.'

The vine that shared the row with the little fig tree felt rather sorry for her. 'That's not quite fair,' it said to the other vine. 'We've got trellises to hold us up, but the fig has had to stand up to the wind all by herself.'

That year the vines produced an even better crop. The wine was praised by everyone who tasted it. The owner came to congratulate the caretaker and to see if the fig tree had some fruit. He looked rather peeved at seeing only leaves again. 'She needs a bit more time,' the caretaker told him. 'Next year, probably.'

Again the months passed, the earth rested, and then fruiting season arrived. As the grapes began to bulge, the vines stared at the fig tree. The one two rows down could scarcely contain its contempt. 'Fruitless again? You're a total waste of space. If I were the owner, I'd pull you up and plant more of us. Our wine was the best in the region last year, and it was only our second crop.'

The fig tree was silent. The vines had taken everything the soil had that year, leaving her bereft of figs. But she could feel her roots wrapped around the deeper rock and spreading out through the soil. She could even feel some of her roots curling around the trellises nearest her, entwined with the vines. She knew her branches were strong enough to hold fruit and that she would be able to face the worst of storms, but for now, she would have to brave the bitter winds of ridicule.

This time, though, when the owner came for figs, he was really annoyed. 'It's just using up the soil and doing nothing,' he told the caretaker. 'Cut it down.'

'Give her one more year,' answered the caretaker. 'I'll dig some fertiliser around her roots. Perhaps she's having a tough time in amongst all the vines.'

That year, as the months passed between fruiting seasons, the caretaker spread fertiliser around the base of the fig tree and watered it in. 'There you are,' he said to the little tree. 'I know you've got tough competition, but do your best.'

As the weeks went by, the fig tree began to feel that she had a chance. Her roots were deep, her branches were strong, and thanks to the fertiliser, she could finally feel tiny bumps growing. Figs at last!

Then one night, just as the vines were beginning their usual boast about the size of their grapes, the storm hit. Hurricane-force winds swept through the valley, driving huge lumps of hail through the vineyard. They ripped and battered the vines, pulverising their fruit. Just before dawn, a violent gust of wind hit the trellises. With splintering sounds rising above even the roar of the wind, they crashed into each other, ripping the vines from the earth.

Later that morning, the landowner and the caretaker came to find out what happened. As they wandered through the field, all they could see was devastation. The caretaker felt despair. Looking after the vines was his livelihood, and now that they were only fit for the fire, he was sure he would lose his job. But as they walked further down the field, they stopped, amazed. All the vines and trellises lay in ruins—all except for one vine that shared its row with the little fig tree, and the two rows either side.

'What do you think,' asked the owner, 'could it be worth salvaging?'

'Definitely,' answered the caretaker. 'We could create a new market for fig and grape wine.'

As they left to discuss it, the remaining vines wrapped their shallow roots closely around the fig's. 'Thank you,' they whispered. 'Thank you for saving us. We felt you straining to hold on to all of us as well. But why, after we'd made things so hard for you? Why didn't you just let us die?'

The fig tree stretched her branches towards the vines, glad of the gentler wind that ruffled her leaves. 'How could I have let go of you when the caretaker would never have given up on me?'

You are the One
who has searched for us
across all the aeons
of our abandonment of You.

Faithful to Your self-crucifying dreams,
You have loved us into life.

# 7

## FAITHFULNESS

From the time she had been a small child, Karen had dreamed great dreams. Soaring in her mind, she had been the saviour. Each time her war-torn father's demons had stuck a burning pitchfork into her shell-shocked self-worth, she had been the pilot who safely landed the stricken aircraft, saving everyone on board. Whenever her mother had suppressed her own losses by needling her with intramuscular mockery, Karen had been the one who rescued a child lost in a cave, blinking into the light of cheering, grateful crowds.

Though Karen walked through the valley of others' shadows, her imagination overflowed. Through so many heroic rescues, the dreams of saving others became her own salvation. As long as childhood wounds could remain hidden, fantasy feared no evil, and she imagined her soul restored.

Then came the moment one cold, misty morning when a taunting little voice of reality whispered, 'All you've ever done is dream. You imagine you've helped so many, but it's only been in your mind. What have you actually done? How many more years will you waste on a lie?'

On the far side of the catatonic hours that followed, Karen finally remembered to breathe. With her means of survival exposed as the grandiosity of skydiving without a parachute, she plummeted into the freezing waters of shame. As belittlement unconsciously fled in search of redemption, her yearnings to save, and therefore to be loved and valued, sifted through her harvest of fantasies. Yet flowing through them was a deeper need. She longed to truly be of the Light; to be one through whom God's blessedness could flow. For so long pretensions had protectively buried her pain, but now, as heartbreak cried out for relief, she vowed that one of the grand dreams, at least, she would make real.

This had to be a gift from heaven. As she opened the letter offering her the job of temporary lighthouse keeper, Karen felt almost dizzy with excitement. In a rush of imaginings, huge passenger liners were kept from disembowelling themselves, but this dream, Karen believed, was anchored to real possibility. Although the lighthouse was derelict and unlikely to be replaced, it was still on a dangerous stretch of coastline. Although it was an isolated post, there would be help and support.

The letter promised a supply boat would come each week. It would bring food, mail, and kerosene to keep the antiquated lamp burning. In an emergency there was a phone link to the coastguard. Once a month she would be relieved for four days by a local volunteer. The poor pay only added to Karen's sense of purpose. Although she had been the only applicant, her sense of calling to a vital work beamed undiminished across the headland of her heart. As she wrote her letter of acceptance, Karen knew that her moment had finally come. No matter what happened, she would prove herself trustworthy. Faithfully she would guard the light as it streaked its silent warning across the bows of treachery's power.

❧

It took nearly five weeks for Karen to realise, and then to accept, that the promises were as insubstantial as the fluffy clouds. She had been brought to the lighthouse in a boat laden with supplies, but since then she had been entirely alone. On this wild and remote length of coast, anyone without a car was stranded. No other boat had come. After the initial ten days she had tried to contact the coastguard but discovered the phone had been disconnected.

With trustful hopefulness singing a lullaby to anxiety, she had waited for the first volunteer, thinking that there must have been a change of plans. Perhaps supplies and help would all be coming overland.

Yet as the sun rose over the fourth day of the fifth week, its rays impaled Karen on a shaft of sudden, despairing comprehension. No one was coming. Whatever had gone wrong, she had been abandoned. As the salty waves frothed over the rocks below, Karen wrapped her hands around another cup of coffee and diluted it with her tears.

As the next two days paced like caged, hungry lions waiting for release, Karen locked her disappointment in a den of practicalities. She anticipated that, if she were very careful, she could stretch the food supply a further six weeks. She could cope with the lack of a break by trying to sleep more during the day. There was cleaning to be done and small repairs to work on, but as she checked the kerosene levels, her greatest concern was for the light.

With autumn lengthening the hours of darkness, each night would call for more fuel. While she could limit her own food each day, the needs of the lamp would only increase. In what had felt like destiny's arms, Karen had vowed faithfully to tend the light, to keep it alive, to keep everyone safe.

Now, as reality left her bereft, all her losses, with sudden tsunami force, surged over the barrier of survival's strength. With fantasy a sham and no other means of escape, Karen crawled into a corner, trying not to drown in the depths of her pain.

❧

In many acidic ways, exclusion had seared her life. The biting humiliations of childhood. The unnamed aching for affirmation which was so belittling. The affection-starved groping for love as a young adult that had flashed innocent need across the radar screens of the predatory. The times of reaching out, and being reached for, only to be used and ditched. Silently, in the guise of grief, its torturing message had branded her spirit with, 'You don't matter. You don't count. No one really cares about you. You are nothing.'

Shivering beneath the threadbare security blanket of her dreams, Karen created compensation, of sorts. Now, with reality's ruthlessness having abandoned her to an impossible task, she recognised the sour taste in her mouth as resentment. Anger, she had long since befriended. This insidious creeper was a corroding enemy she knew she had to defeat, and she had three weeks.

That there were just three weeks before the kerosene ran out was her estimation. Battling resentment with the power of choice, Karen stared into the abyss of her pain, and abandonment blinked first. She would stay. She would hold out as long as she could. For God, and for anyone out there in the dark, she would tend the light. Despite all the disappointment and betrayal, she would remain faithful. Let down and alone, she would still hold the light for as long as she possibly could.

The day after the fuel ran out, a storm crashed into land. In sinister slowness it had been growing and threatening. Karen had tried to make the kerosene last a bit longer by turning the lamp on and off, but finally the light had sputtered into oblivion. As far as she knew, no ship had come anywhere near in the time that she had been there. But now, as huge waves exploded between the rocks, she heard it.

Even above the raging wind, the boat's siren carried the mournful message of its presence. With panic screaming its urgency, Karen grabbed the only source of light she had left—her little torch—and slithered down the cliff path onto the rocks. Somehow she had to make the light visible. Somehow she had to keep the boat safely away.

Casting arcs of torchlight, for just a few moments Karen was able to keep her footing, but there was nothing to hold onto. With waves flinging themselves in her face, one massive wave finally caught her. It flung her flailing into the foam. But in that moment, the sky suddenly erupted with lightning. Her tiny torchlight gone, great shafts of blazing light lit the coastline for miles.

Certain that she was about to drown, Karen struggled desperately to breathe. And as the lightning slashed across the surface of the sea, it was just long enough for her to see the life buoy. As another wave jostled her, it swept her closer. Reaching out, she sobbed her relief as she managed to cling to the buoy and felt herself being pulled towards the boat.

Later, as Karen wrapped her hands around a cup of coffee, the coastguard member was profuse in his apologies. He had offered to deliver the supplies and to make sure that she had everything she needed. But of the two lighthouses due for closure along that coast, he had assumed that Karen was taken to the more reliable one. Thinking each time that she had gone for a walk, he had just left the supplies. Someone must have taken them.

How Karen had kept that rickety old lamp burning he could not imagine. When he finally heard where she was and had seen the gathering storm, he had set out immediately to bring her back, but with the mountainous waves, he had struggled to get there in time. Thank God for the lightning. What a blessing she had just held onto the buoy and let herself be rescued. Thank God, most of all, for that faithful old boat. Without it, he would never have reached Karen in time. Small and unremarkable it might be, but he had lost count of how many its siren of hope had saved.

How is it that it is only woundedness
that is the cradle of new birth—
only relentless pain?

Why not a dancing, colourful mobile
with horses and frogs, butterflies and fairies,
and sudden, juice-bursting moments
of unpretentious joy?

In fire, we are flayed,
and in ashes we grovel for crumbs.
Is it only the phoenix, then,
that truly learns to fly?

# 8

## GENTLENESS, HUMILITY

All was at peace across the colony. The sun, slowly surrendering to twilight, left streaks of fire for the night to weave into dawn. A few younger birds nudged each other from the rocks for a final swim, but most had settled to sleep.

One small one, however, refused rest. Having wedged herself into a slit in a rock out of sight of the others, she stared at the water—across, beyond, far into the mists of her imagining. A shadow of fluff and frailty, she suffered the memory of what happened the day before.

Such grace and magnificence had seemed not of this world; certainly far from hers for penguins cannot fly. Out of the vastness of ocean's reach she had come as though one who would bring water through hell to a withering weed. She had come seeking the little penguin, come with such hope and such power. Now the chick huddled deeper into the rock, wearied from the forces of the choice she now faced.

⌘

The albatross had watched the penguin colony for many days before her visit. She had especially watched the little, lonely one who always stayed in a rock slit, staring out to sea, unimpressed by the numbers of fish the others caught. Each day the chick watched birds flying over the rocks, masters of the wind's command. Their freedom made a torment of even the racing of her heart. Silently she screamed at the air that would never carry her and fumed at the injustice that pins penguins to the ground.

She watched the older ones waddling across the rocks, stunted wings flapping their mockery, and cursed the thought of time's ageing that would make her like them. Hidden in her rock, the chick flew in her mind. Her days were absorbed in dreams of clouds she would never know the chill of and great trees on which she would never look down. So to the little one, the albatross had come. Now, as darkness made ghosts of the light of her dreams, she stumbled through her own darkness, trying to remain unseen.

⌘

Unnoticed by the other penguins, the albatross had left the sky's wings for the aching in forbidding rock. The quiet intensity of her eyes had made the chick shrink back in sudden exposure. At first she had said nothing. Then, 'Tell me, little one, what is your name?'

'I'm too young to have lived the meaning of a name. When I am seven moons old it will be chosen, but for now, I am called by the star of my birth.'

The albatross had looked at her, head to one side. 'Why is it that you're here, in a rock, having no part in anything that the others do?'

'They're happy to swim and boast of their white chests to other birds who don't care.'

'And you are not?'

'No. I want to fly.'

'That's not the way of penguins. Why would you fly rather than swim?' the albatross had asked.

'I don't really know,' the penguin chick answered. 'It's just that, from here, all there is, is cold greyness and endless sea. I feel the echo of something far away, beyond me yet all around. Without wings it's always out of reach—calling, taunting, knowing I can never come.'

'Perhaps you can,' the albatross had said quietly.

'But how?'

The albatross had moved closer. 'Get on my back, and I'll show you.'

Hesitantly, yet somehow certain that she could trust this strange, awesome bird, the chick had scrambled onto the albatross's wing and across into the deeper body feathers.

'Ready?'

'I think so.'

'Hold onto me, and don't be afraid.'

The chick had felt a release of power and cool air flowing over her eyes. At first she had dug her feet hard into the albatross's back, afraid to look. But then, with a surge of curiosity and excitement, she raised her head from the feathers to look below. In an instant, she felt as though her heart had turned inside out to fall trembling against the extremity of her longing. The sight had stunned her. Far below, the sea had stretched seemingly into oblivion in three shades of blue. Clouds had played tag with the sun to send streaks of shadow across the waves.

The albatross drifted close to the surface of the water to show her a shoal of tiny fish. Then, with a slight tilt of her wings, she had altered direction to fly inland. Feeling slightly creepy inside, the chick had closed her eyes for a moment. When she looked again everything had changed. 'The water has turned into feathers!'

'No, little one. That's grass.'

'Does it hurt?'

'No. It's soft to walk in, and many tiny animals live in its shelter.'

The chick looked at it more carefully. 'Why doesn't it move?'

'Part of it must always be inside the earth. Otherwise it would die. You'll see very soon.'

The little chick had lived the next hour in a spray of excitement, exploring the field, finding so many things unknown to penguins. As she had wandered back to the waiting albatross, one discovery had quietened her. 'It *does* move. Just the top part, the end we can see. It bends when the wind touches it, but none of it gets blown away. Why are there places with no grass?'

The albatross had looked sad and had not answered. Within what had seemed like seconds, the little penguin had been returned to the colony. Even the strength of the flying wind had not been able to muffle the albatross's words. 'There is much more to see, to learn, to understand. I can take you from this rock. You can fly always with me, but for a time so that I can teach you, you must stay as small as you are now while your longings grow and your dreams expand. If your body outgrows your heart, I shall not be able to hold you. You must decide. Soon I shall return. For now, be at peace, and farewell.'

In half a blink, the albatross had gone, leaving the chick bewildered and overwhelmed, yet tingling through her fluff with the wonder of wind-speed.

The little penguin could barely understand her confusion. Always before, the adult penguins had seemed so clumsy. Their existence had seemed so restricted, and she would gladly have changed into any other kind of bird. Now, as she watched them through the retreating light, the little one suddenly wanted to be taller, to have a white chest and feathers. Her own soft down was the brand of infancy and brought no respect. If she managed to grow more feathers than most, a sharper beak, and bigger feet, she might even become colony leader. Hers would be the power to command. Some would catch her fish for her, while others would count it an honour to preen her magnificent feathers. She would gaze out from a high rock while penguins near and far scurried to do her bidding. She would have to be big and imposing. No one would listen to a mere chick.

As she sat, fevered brooding spiralled slowly upwards to a seizure of frustration. Its coils squeezed and choked, and in the urgency of newborn rebellion, she tumbled out of her niche, blundered across the rocks, and struggled to the top of the highest one she could find. *I don't need an albatross,* she thought. *I can do this myself. I can grow as big as any of the others, and fly. The nothingness of air will not dare to drop me. I'll be the only flying penguin. I shall be named as no other for no other will have lived my name. The old ones will bow their heads to me, and chicks will scatter from my path in awe. I shall be unfettered and free—a legend on wings!*

Clenching her eyes shut in desperate defiance, she dived. The wings that had carried her to glory in her mind beat helplessly as she crashed onto the rocks many feet below.

The inward tide spilled into the rock pool, renewing its blood-mingled water from a groaning sea. The coldness of a smaller wave reached out and touched the chick. She stirred, but a huge weight of dizziness seemed to glue her head to the rock.

Even to open her eyes was painful. She lay still, a broken huddle of blood-soaked fluff waiting for death to drown her shame.

'Asheran.'

Barely a whisper, the voice silenced the power of time's burden of words. It commanded death to come forth from the grave, yet it came to the chick as gently as the first probe of sunlight from which dense murk could choose to flee.

'My little one, did you not understand? To fly with me it is just the wings of your heart that need to grow.

'I thought there could be another way. Why do you bother with me? It's too late now. As daylight comes, so will my life be gone, and no one will have noticed or cared.'

The albatross brushed the chick with her wing tip. 'No. That cannot be now for I have given you a name, one that you will live. You are Asheran.'

'What does it mean?' whispered the chick.

'Its meaning is in that it has no meaning, alone. It is part of my name, which I give to you. Only as you give it back to me will you know who you are for then you will know who I am.'

The great bird drew in her wings and covered the chick until all awareness of the night was lost in a different kind of darkness. Through it, she could feel the pain fading into a faraway memory. Without knowing how, the chick found herself, once more, enfolded in the albatross's wing feathers. And as the days passed, many penguins of distant colonies stopped fishing to watch the strange sight of an albatross gliding over the rocks with a penguin chick, stubby wings outstretched, riding on her back.

When they finally disappeared, the penguins soon forgot about them and went back to their fishing, All save one little chick, who sat in a rock slit, in awe of a strange bird that had come. Gently she had said to the chick, 'You can fly with me always, but for a time, you must stay as small as you are now while your longings grow and your dreams expand.' A chick who, though stunned, had been filled with wonder. For though this bird had the wings of an albatross, her eyes had shone with the laughter of a penguin.

An acorn
can only grow into an oak;
the frond
can only unfurl as a fern.

As seeds of God,
we alone are given the terrifying gift
of choosing what we will become.

# 9

## SELF-CONTROL

It had been a dreadful day for Oliver. He had gone to bed feeling reasonable enough, but whatever had gone on during the night, he had woken feeling tired and grumpy. So early on, he had given himself permission to have a bad day. *I'm only human,* he thought. *Everyone can move over for me today.*

Evidently his car had not been listening. He went out to the garage and found one of its tyres was flat. Oliver's allocation of straws for this day had been non-existent; he had sucked on his last straw in one breath. Slamming the garage door shut, he stormed inside and phoned for a taxi to take him to the station.

Creeping through the early traffic, the taxi had only taken four minutes longer than he had been assured it would take, but Oliver had been in no mood to be forgiving. All the way to the station he had let fly about the state of services in general, and the taxi service in particular, insinuating none too subtly that he held his driver personally responsible for it all. Feeling considerably better, he had got out of the taxi and walked across to the platform.

By the time he had got on the train, Oliver had decided that what he really wanted was space. He just needed a day with no more problems, no demands, nobody wanting something by last week. So when his mobile phone had rung and he had seen that it was his daughter, he just let it ring. She had just moved into a new flat, and most of her calls were, 'Dad, can you fix the cupboard door?' or, 'Dad, can you come and unblock the sink?' More often, though, it was, 'Dad, can you lend me £100? I'll pay it back, promise!' Well not today. It was time she learned to stand on her own feet.

By lunchtime, Oliver had decided to get away. He took his sandwiches and found a seat under a tree in the park. There were less people there than usual—a couple of joggers, a woman with a pram, and a child who seemed to be playing by herself on the swings. As he watched, a man had approached the child and seemed to be trying to persuade her to go with him. She had obviously been reluctant, and as the man picked her up and walked quickly to his car, the child had started crying and hitting him.

Something about the whole situation had made Oliver feel uneasy, but he brushed it aside. It had been yet another intrusion into a rotten day when he was just trying to find a bit of peace. Reminding himself of his daughter's tantrums when she was ever taken away from something she was enjoying, he tossed his lunch wrappings vaguely in the direction of the rubbish bin and walked slowly back to work.

After an afternoon of indulging his decision to have a bad day, ensuring that everyone else had one as well, he slammed the door on his colleagues and went home. Only then had he heard about the accident. His daughter was in hospital in a coma with multiple injuries after a car accident in which two people had died.

When Oliver eventually got to bed in the small hours of the morning, he had a dream. He saw himself getting out of a taxi, still abusing the driver, slamming the door, and walking towards the station. The dream then turned towards the taxi driver. Just before he set off for work that morning, he had received a letter saying that a close friend had died. Still in shock from the news, he drove to pick up his first fare only to have Oliver verbally mug him. He felt so upset and angry that, ten minutes later, he lost concentration and had to swerve to avoid hitting another car. As a result, he hit a dog sitting in a driveway before crashing into a tree.

In his dream, Oliver's daughter, Jane, came running out of the house. She saw that the driver was only shaken but that her dog was severely injured. She desperately tried to phone her dad on his mobile, but it seemed to be switched off. Realising that she would have to try to get her dog to the vet by herself, she picked him up as carefully as she could and put him in the car.

Driving down the road, she was so distracted by her dog's distress that she missed seeing the red light at the roadwork. As she slammed into the car in front, it was shunted into the path of the oncoming cars. In the six-car pile-up, Jane had head injuries and multiple fractures; two people in the oncoming car were killed instantly.

One of those was a young mother who had told her daughter to stay by the school gate until she came to collect her at lunchtime as the school had a half-day. Little Gemma waited while everyone else was collected, assuring other mothers that hers was coming. In the happy confusion of parents picking up their children, no one noticed Gemma picking up her bag.

She had decided to walk home, but on the way, she saw the swings. Gemma loved swings. It was like flying. She ran over and climbed on. There was a man standing nearby who looked at her in a way that made her feel strange and uneasy. But there was another man not too far away eating his sandwiches, so she knew she would be safe. It was a man Oliver immediately recognised. He saw him every time he looked in the mirror.

As he dreamed, feeling ever more sick and appalled, a messenger came and sat beside him.

'It's all my fault,' Oliver gasped, despairingly. 'I can't believe I caused all that.'

'Well,' said the messenger, 'you couldn't have known what would happen. But you did have some choices. It was yours to decide who you would be that day.'

'But I felt so rotten when I woke up,' replied Oliver. 'We're all human. We all have bad days.'

'I know,' said the messenger. 'But that day may have been the only one you had.'

As he dreamed, the messenger left him. Oliver woke to light cascading through his bedroom window, and the sound of a rumpus outside his door. He was still blinking awake when Jane burst in and bounced onto the bed beside him.

'Wake up, Dad,' she said excitedly. 'I've got something great to show you.'

The next minute a small bundle of wiggle was leaping all over him, the little dog's tongue trying to do the job of a razor on his face.

'Isn't he wonderful? I just got him yesterday. I tried to let you know we were coming, but you must have had your phone turned off.'

Blinking back tears, Oliver realised that it had all been a dream—that whole, terrible day. His real day was just beginning. Even though he felt exhausted, the sun was warm on his face.

'By the way, Dad,' said Jane, 'I noticed on the way in that your car's got a flat tyre. Shall I give you a lift to work?'

For freedom Christ has set us free.
The fruit of the Spirit is love, joy, peace, patience,
kindness, goodness, faithfulness, gentleness and self-control.
If we live by the Spirit, let us also be guided by the Spirit.

Galatians 5:1, 22, 25

*Translations from the Greek*

Love, goodwill, kindly concern, generosity, devotedness.

Joy, delight, gladness, rejoicing, bliss.

Peace, freedom from war, concord between people.
Everything that makes for a person's
highest good. Tranquillity of heart.

Patience, longsuffering, forbearance,
fortitude, patient expectation.

Kindness, uprightness, gentleness.

Goodness, virtue.

Faithfulness, trustworthiness.

Gentleness, humility, being considerate.

Self-control, temperance.

Printed and bound by CPI Group (UK) Ltd, Croydon, CR0 4YY